Little Grey Rabbit's Birthday

by Alison Uttley

Pictures by Margaret Tempest

COLLINS COLOUR CUBS

Squirrel and Hare were gardening one fine day. Squirrel was sowing dandelions and Hare was watering them.

"It's little Grey Rabbit's birthday on Midsummer Day," said Squirrel, as she shook the dandelion clocks and let the seeds fly.

"I think it's time for my birthday," pondered Hare. "It's weeks and weeks since I had a birthday."

"It isn't your turn, Hare. Grey Rabbit hasn't had a birthday for a whole year. We must give her a nice present."

"Of course," agreed Hare. "A cake or something. Yes, something we can all share."

"Yes. A birthday cake with candles on it," said Squirrel.

"I don't like the taste of candles," objected Hare.

"They're not to eat!" cried Squirrel. "They are to show how old you are. Three candles if you are three years old."

"And a hundred if you are a hundred years old," said Hare, "Oh, Squirrel, can we make the cake ourselves?"

"I think so," nodded Squirrel. "We can't ask Grey Rabbit to make it. It must be a secret."

Just then Grey Rabbit came running out of the house.

"Oh Squirrel!" she cried. "I asked you to sow lettuce seed and you are putting dandelions in the garden. Another gardener will sow them for us."

"Who's that?" asked Squirrel.

"The wind," said Grey Rabbit. "He'll plant dandelion seeds."

"Grey Rabbit!" interrupted Hare. "Squirrel and I have been saying that your b-b-- that it will be your b-b--"

"Hist! Never a word!" whispered Squirrel.

"No! Never a word! It's a secret," said Hare hastily.

"A secret from me?" asked Grey Rabbit.

"We can't tell you. It wouldn't be a secret if you knew," explained Squirrel.

"No, we can't speak it. It's something that mustn't be told," added Hare with importance. But the secret was just about to hop out of Hare's mouth, when Squirrel rushed at him with a handkerchief and tied him up.

"Have you got toothache?" asked Grey Rabbit.

Hare shook his head, but not a word could he utter.

"Will you come for a walk to visit the Speckledy Hen?" asked Grey Rabbit. "I want some eggs for tea."

"We'll come won't we, Hare?" said Squirrel, throwing down her rake.

"Mum-mum-mum-m-m!" grunted Hare.

They went through the field where Moldy Warp lived.

Moldy Warp was sitting in his house, smoking his pipe. "Hello!" he cried when the three friends arrived. "This is a surprise."

He hurried to fetch glasses of heather ale, and brought them outside.

"Oh dear! Have you got toothache, Hare?" he asked.

"No. He's keeping a secret," explained Squirrel.

Hare looked at the heather ale and he looked at Squirrel, till Mole took pity on him and untied the knot.

"I'm going to tell," he exclaimed. "I can't keep it in. I shall burst if I tell nobody."

"No! No!" cried Squirrel, shaking his arm.

"Come inside, and whisper to me and the doorpost," said Mole kindly. Hare followed him into the passage, and then he spoke up.

"It's Grey Rabbit's birthday on Midsummer Day, and we are going to make a cake," he said breathlessly.

"Ah! That is a good secret!" agreed Mole. "I'll give her a present."

"And come to tea with us," said Hare, "and taste the cake."

"Thank you, Hare," said Mole. "I don't think I need tie you up again. You won't tell Grey Rabbit, now you've told me and the doorpost."

The three friends said good-bye to Moldy Warp, and Grey Rabbit led the way through the edge of the wood.

In the distance was the great beech tree that was Owl's house. They looked at the silver bell, but were afraid to pull it. So Squirrel ran up the tree and called softly through the open window.

"Wise Owl! Wise Owl! It's Grey Rabbit's birthday on Midsummer Day."

"Gr-gr-gr," snored Wise Owl, but he heard in his dreams all the same.

They passed into the fields where Milkman Hedgehog was coming back from milking.

"Can we have a drink?" asked Squirrel, dancing up to him. "It's thirsty work keeping secrets."

Hare took old Hedgehog aside and whispered to him:

"It's Grey Rabbit's birthday on Midsummer Day. We are going to make her a cake, and you can come and taste it."

"Ah! Thank ye!" cried Hedgehog. "I'll make a tiddly present for Miss Grey Rabbit."

"Come along, Hare. We shall never get to the Speckledy Hen's house," called Grey Rabbit, "if you spend all the time telling secrets."

When they arrived at the farm, there was the Speckledy Hen walking out with her little sunshade over her head.

"We've come for some eggs, Speckledy Hen," said Grey Rabbit. While the Hen was filling up the basket, Hare went and whispered in her ear.

"It's Grey Rabbit's birthday on Midsummer Day. We are going to make a cake and you can come and taste it."

"I'll bring a present for dear Grey Rabbit," whispered the Hen. "And mind you put plenty of eggs in the cake, Hare."

The next day Squirrel and Hare decided to make the cake.

"We must get Grey Rabbit out of the way and do it secretly," said Hare. "Won't she be surprised! She doesn't know we can make cakes."

"We don't know either," muttered Squirrel. She was doubtful, but Hare was full of confidence.

"Grey Rabbit! Grey Rabbit! Go away! We don't want you!" commanded Hare sternly.

Grey Rabbit came in from the garden.

"Oh Hare! What have I done? What's the matter." Her ears drooped, and a tear came to her eye. Why was there such a mystery?

Squirrel stamped her foot.

"Hare! How stupid you are!"

She wiped Grey Rabbit's eyes and then spoke kindly to her.

"Grey Rabbit! Will you please take a bottle of primrose wine to Wise Owl? Moldy Warp would like a visit, and I'm sure Fuzzypeg would love to hear a story."

"I'll run off at once," said Grey Rabbit, smiling at the two friends.

"Good-bye! Don't hurry back," called Squirrel and Hare, and they waved their paws as Grey Rabbit went along the lane.

"Quickly! Quickly!" cried Hare, and they bounded into the house.

Squirrel sprang on the dresser and sniffed at all the jars of spices and herbs.

"Here's tansy and woodruff, and preserved violets, and bottled cherries," said she.

"Here's fern-seed and poppy-seed, and acorns and beech-nuts," said Hare. "Oh, here's the pepper pot. How much shall I put in?"

"A fistful of everything makes a nice cake," said Squirrel.

So they dipped their paws into every jar, and mixed the seeds and herbs in the yellow bowl.

"Is the oven hot?" said a deep voice, and they both sprang round in alarm. There, at the window, was old Hedgehog watching them with twinkling eyes.

"I comed with extra milk for the cake," said he. "You didn't ought to forget the oven and you didn't ought to put pepper in the cake."

Hare blushed and tried to hide the pepper pot.

"Oh, Hare! How could you! We shall have to begin all over again."

"I'll come and lend a hand," said old Hedgehog. And he made up the fire and gave Hare the blow-bellows to puff the flames. He showed Squirrel how to mix the sugar and butter together and how to sprinkle in the currants and spices.

Hare ran to the garden and brought in rose petals and violets and pinks and clover – all the sweet-smelling things he could find to add to the cake. He beat up the eggs till they were a yellow froth and Hedgehog dropped them into the mixture.

"Now I must be off," said Hedgehog. "Remember not to open the oven door till the good rich smell comes out."

They popped the cake in the oven and shut the door.

After a time there came a strong sweet smell which made Hare wrinkle his nose.

"The cake!" he cried. "It's telling us it's ready to come out."

So Squirrel wrapped a cloth round her paw and lifted out the good-smelling cake.

They carried it into the garden and hid it under an empty beehive.

The next day when Grey Rabbit had gone out to gather wool from the hedges, Squirrel ran to the garden for the cake. She iced it and wrote GREY RABBIT'S BIRTHDAY on the top in pollen dust. Hare went to the cupboard and took out every candle he could find.

They put them all round the edge and then they hid the cake in the beehive again.

"I'm going to make a fan for Grey Rabbit," said Squirrel. "I shall ask the green woodpecker and the goldfinch for some feathers."

"And I will make a purse for her," said Hare.

Squirrel begged a few feathers from the birds. She put them together, and there was the prettiest little fan of green and gold.

Hare went to the pasture for a puff-ball. He squeezed out the dust, and washed the little bag in the dew, then he tied it with ribbon-grasses.

Darkness came and the three little animals went upstairs to bed. In the night Grey Rabbit was wakened by a faint noise under her window. She sat up and listened. Her eyes were wide open.

She slipped out of bed and putting her cloak over her nightgown, she ran downstairs and into the garden. There, crouched in a sad prickly little ball, was Fuzzypeg. "What's the matter, Fuzzypeg?" whispered Grey Rabbit.

"I comed to say Happy Birthday," said Fuzzypeg. "I got out of the window, and I runned very fast, but I heard Wise Owl hooting, and I got frightened."

"Poor little Fuzzypeg," said Grey Rabbit softly. "You had better come into my bed." She took his paw and led him upstairs. He leaped in to the pretty bed and looked round the room.

"Isn't it nice!" he cried. "I knew you'd take care of me, Grey Rabbit. A Happy Birthday, Grey Rabbit."

"It isn't my birthday till tomorrow, Fuzzypeg," said Grey Rabbit.

She tucked him up, then she wrapped her cloak round herself and crept under the bed. She couldn't sleep with a bundle of prickles by her side.

"Grey Rabbit. Is it tomorrow?" he called.

Far away they could hear the church clock strike midnight.

"A Happy Birthday," said Fuzzypeg quickly.

The next morning Hare and Squirrel raced downstairs to get the breakfast.

"I'm going to say Happy Birthday to Grey Rabbit," said Hare.

"So am I," said Squirrel.

So upstairs they bundled, and they flung open the bedroom door.

"Happy Birthday!" came squeaking from the bed. Squirrel and Hare looked at each other.

"*You* don't say it, Grey Rabbit," said Hare. "*We* say it." He gave the bed-clothes a hard pat.

Out of the blankets came Fuzzypeg's dark head.

"Good morning," said he. "I said it first."

The noise wakened Grey Rabbit, and she crawled out from under the bed.

Hare and Squirrel were so surprised they never said "Happy Birthday" at all.

"Milk-o! Milk-o!" the call came from the kitchen. "Has anyone seen our Fuzzypeg? He runned away in the night, and it's my belief he came to see Miss Grey Rabbit."

"Here he is, Hedgehog!" they shouted, running downstairs.

"I said it first," boasted Fuzzypeg. "I said Happy Birthday before any of you."

"He said he would be the first, and he's done it," said old Hedgehog proudly.

"Let him stay for breakfast," pleaded Grey Rabbit, and Hedgehog agreed. Fuzzypeg made some more toast and soon they were sitting round the table.

"It's your birthday, Grey Rabbit," said Squirrel, "so you shall have a holiday. We'll wash the cups and plates and make the beds."

"Then I'll go into the garden with Fuzzypeg and show him the flowers," said Grey Rabbit. When they came to the beehive a stream of honey-bees flew out, and another stream flew in.

"Hare! Squirrel! Come here! A swarm of bees is living in our empty hive," called Grey Rabbit. "Isn't it exciting?"

"Oh! Oh! Oh!" cried Squirrel and Hare. "Oh! What shall we do?" and Squirrel burst into tears.

"Listen," said Grey Rabbit. "The bees are humming something," and this is what the animals heard:

"It's Grey Rabbit's Birthday,
She doesn't want money,
Or fine clothes or riches.
We'll make her some honey."

Hare and Squirrel looked at one another and sighed.

At four o'clock they sent Grey Rabbit upstairs, while they got ready the tea. They ran down the garden to the beehive for the cake. Hare put a butterfly net over his head, lest he should be stung, but the bees had gone.

They lifted up the straw skep, and there was the cake, and around it were many little pots of honey, each as big as a thimble. The pots were made of golden wax and the honey was scented with wild thyme.

They carried the treasures indoors and placed them on the table. Grey Rabbit came running downstairs.

"Oh! Oh!" cried Grey Rabbit. "What's this?"

"It's somebody's birthday cake," said Squirrel.

"It's everybody's cake, and here they come to the feast," said Hare.

Up the path came many little feet. Then there was a rat-tat-tat at the door.

"Come in! Come in!" cried Squirrel. In trooped Moldy Warp, the Hedgehog family, Water Rat, the Speckledy Hen and a crowd of little animals.

"Many Happy Returns, Grey Rabbit," they cried. They saw the table, the lighted cake and the honey pots.

"Oh-oh-oh-oh! It's like Moldy Warp's Christmas tree."

Squirrel gave Grey Rabbit the little fan made of feathers. Hare brought out the purse with green ribbon-grass. Everybody had brought a present; but Moldy Warp's present was the best of all. It was the song of a nightingale in a tiny polished musical box.

They were all listening to the music as Grey Rabbit turned the handle, when the door was pushed open and a round feathered head, and a pair of large blinking eyes appeared.

"I won't come in," hooted Wise Owl, "but I have brought a small token of my regard for Grey Rabbit."

He thrust one claw forward and dropped a book on the table. Then he drifted away as silently as he had come.

"Whew!" exclaimed Moldy Warp. "That was a shock."

"What has he brought?" asked Hare.

"It's called 'Wise Owl's Guide to Knowledge'," said Grey Rabbit, holding the tiny green volume.

"Cut the cake, Grey Rabbit!" called Hare. "I'm hungry. Cut the cake!"

So Grey Rabbit cut the beautiful birthday cake and they all had a piece. It was as nice as it looked.

Moldy Warp drank Grey Rabbit's health, and Water Rat made a speech. Squirrel recited a little poem and Hare played a tune on his flute.

They all laughed and sang and danced till night came, and then they went home by the light of the moon.

"What a lovely birthday it has been," said Grey Rabbit. "How kind everybody is to me."

She looked at her presents on the table: the musical box with the song of the nightingale, Wise Owl's 'Guide to Knowledge', a handkerchief from Mrs Hedgehog, a tiny chestnut basket of flowers from Fuzzypeg, a little canoe from Water Rat, the feather fan, the puff-ball purse, the honey pots, and all the other little treasures.

She went upstairs to bed, with the musical box under her arm. She turned the handle and the voice of the nightingale came trilling forth. From the woods another nightingale answered.

"A Happy Birthday, Grey Rabbit,"
it seemed to say.

Alison Uttley's original story has been
abridged for this book. The thirty Little Grey
Rabbit books are still available in hardback
editions.

ISBN 0 00 194196 8
Text Copyright © John Uttley 1978
Illustrations Copyright © Margaret Tempest 1978
Printed in Great Britain